This book
belongs to:

....

To Cosmo, Pickle and Princess Cupcake,
my favourite hounds. - BD

For Manon, thanks for letting me sleep
so well to illustrate this book! - CA

LITTLE TIGER PRESS
1 The Coda Centre, 189 Munster Road, London SW6 6AW
www.littletiger.co.uk
First published in Great Britain 2017
Text by Becky Davies • Text copyright © Little Tiger Press 2017
Illustrations copyright © Caroline Attia 2017
Photographs used under license from Shutterstock.com

Caroline Attia has asserted her right to be
identified as the illustrator of this work under
the Copyright, Designs and Patents Act, 1988

A CIP catalogue record for this book is
available from the British Library

The Three Little PUGS and the Big Bad CAT

Becky Davies

Caroline Attia

LITTLE TIGER PRESS
London

Once upon a time, there were three little pugs called Bubbles, Bandit and Beauty. They lived with their mother in a tiny kennel in the woods.

"You three aren't puppies any more," said Mother Pug. "It's time you went to build houses of your own."

What kind of houses shall we build?

Take these snacks and watch out for the Big Bad Cat. She's the meanest moggy around, and will do anything for food. Build strong houses to keep that clever kitty out.

So off the three little pugs went, their backpacks bulging with biscuits.

Bandit and Beauty bounded ahead, while Bubbles dragged his paws at the back.

"I'm starving!"

he wailed, plonking himself down on the ground.
"Can't I just eat a *couple* of treats?"
"You have to build a house first. Remember the **Big Bad Cat!**" warned Beauty.

Come back here, tail!

"Fine," said Bubbles, looking around. "Then I'll build my house right here out of . . . this straw." And that's exactly what he did.

As soon as Bubbles had finished building his straw house, he turned greedily to his treats, licking his little puggy lips.

He opened his mouth as **wide** as it would go, but before he could take a bite, he heard a noise outside.

"Humph! Can't a pug enjoy his biscuits in peace?" snorted Bubbles, and he waddled over to the window to take a look.

Uh-oh!

What a sight!
Sharp scratchy claws,
a terrible **twitching** tail
and **mean** moggy eyes.

"Then I'll **huff**, and I'll **puff**, and I'll **blow** your house down!"

cried the cat, pulling out a hairdryer.

"And I'll barely have to lift a paw."

Holy pugmoly!

It was the Big Bad Cat!
"Little pug, little pug,
let me come in!"
yowled the Big Bad Cat.
"N . . . not by the hairs
on my chinny chin chin!"
trembled Bubbles,
scrambling to
cover his snacks.

The hairdryer whirred ...

and it whooshed ...

and it BLEW THE HOUSE DOWN!

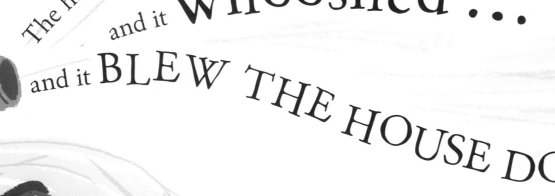

"Yikes!" yelped Bubbles,
and he scurried away
as fast as he could.

Meanwhile, Bandit and Beauty had come across a heap of sticks. "Look, Beauty," panted Bandit. "STICKS! Sticks are my favourite! I could build my **whole house** out of sticks!"

They don't look very strong. What about the Big Bad Cat?

But Bandit wouldn't listen. He ran around happily, chewing sticks, digging holes and building himself a messy little stick house.

Bandit had said goodbye to Beauty and was just about to gobble up his first biscuit when Bubbles hurtled through his front door, wheezing.

"The Big Bad Cat . . ." panted Bubbles. "Coming . . . this way . . . protect the treats!"

But just then, a giant shadow fell across the window. Huddled together, the pugs looked out to see . . .

Sharp scratchy claws, a terrible twitching tail and mean moggy eyes.

Holy pugmoly!
It was the Big Bad Cat
again!

"Little pugs, little pugs, let me come in!" howled the Big Bad Cat.

"N . . . not by the hairs on our chinny chin chins!" trembled Bubbles and Bandit.

"Then I'll huff, and I'll puff, and I'll blow your house down!" the cat declared, pulling out a leaf blower and aiming it at the house of sticks. "And I won't even ruffle my fur," she purred.

The leaf blower spat . . . and it sputtered

Help! My sticks!

Bandit!

Deep in the forest, Beauty had walked and walked until at last she found a pile of bricks. She knew exactly how she'd build her house . . .

Just as the last brick was laid, Bandit and Bubbles came bursting through the trees.

"Beauty! Beauty! The **Big Bad Cat** is coming!" panted Bandit. "She ate our food!" wailed Bubbles. "We're all going to starve!"

"Don't worry, everything is under control," said Beauty, as she gathered her brothers into a huddle. "It's time for plan B, boys! Now listen carefully . . ."

TOP SECRET PLAN 'B

When the **Big Bad Cat** reached the brick house, all was quiet. Too quiet.

"Little pugs, little pugs, let me come in!" growled the cat. But there was no response.

She peeked inside to see . . .

a **bulging** backpack, and three, pug-shaped lumps on the sofa.

"It's no good hiding," the Big Bad Cat purred smugly, "I'll still huff, and I'll puff, and I'll blow your house down! And I shan't even tangle a whisker." She pulled out a giant fan and pointed it at the brick house.

The fan blustered... and it blasted...

but the house stood firm. This would call for something more powerful . . .

...like A JUMBO JET!

The engines revved...

and they roared...

and the door to the brick house blew **right open.**

The Big Bad Cat strutted inside, victorious.
But the backpack was full of sticks!
And the lumps on the sofa were nothing
but cushions!

The Big Bad Cat was FURIOUS.
She yowled and she howled,
she hissed and she spat,
her eyes narrowed, her
tail twitched and she
stamped her paws until . . .

"Muffin!"
trilled a voice through the trees.
"Oh, MUFFIN! Din-dins!"

With a flick of her tail, the cat trotted back home
through the wood, discarding her disguises.

"There you are, my ickle MUFFIN MONSTER!"
said Mrs Honeybun, scooping her up.

"I have the most wonderful surprise for my PRETTY-WITTY
MUFFY-WUFFY. Come with me, PRINCESS."
And she carried her inside the house.

"Look who's joining the family! I just know you're going to be the BEST of FRIENDS!"

And the three little pugs and the Big Bad Cat lived happily ever after . . . well, **almost!**

More **outrageously** funny tales from Little Tiger Press!

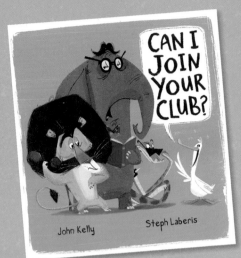

CAN I JOIN YOUR CLUB?

John Kelly · Steph Laberis

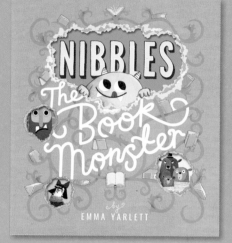

NIBBLES The Book Monster

by EMMA YARLETT

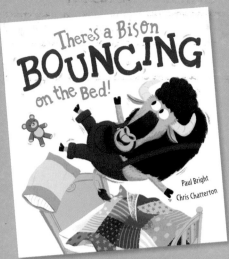

There's a Bison BOUNCING on the Bed!

Paul Bright · Chris Chatterton

Stella J Jones · Judi Abbot

With glitter on every page!

GLITTER

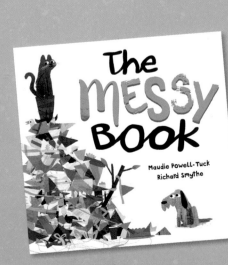

The MESSY BOOK

Maudie Powell-Tuck · Richard Smythe

For information regarding any of the above titles
or for our catalogue, please contact us:
Little Tiger Press, 1 The Coda Centre,
189 Munster Road, London SW6 6AW
Tel: 020 7385 6333 • E-mail: contact@littletiger.co.uk
www.littletiger.co.uk